THOMAS EDISON

CARMEL REILLY

Australia • Brazil • Japan • Korea • Mexico • Singapore • Spain • United Kingdom • United States

Thomas Edison

Fast Forward
Green Level 12

Text: Carmel Reilly
Illustrations: Boris Silvestri
Editor: Johanna Rohan
Design: Vonda Pestana
Series design: James Lowe
Production controller: Emma Hayes
Photo research: Gillian Cardinal
Audio recordings: Juliet Hill, Picture Start
Spoken by: Matthew King and Abbe Holmes

Acknowledgements
The author and publisher would like to acknowledge permission to reproduce material from the following sources: Photographs by Australian Picture Library/Corbis, pp 6, 9/Michael Freeman, back cover, p15/Bettamnn, pp 17 left, 20, 21 right, 23/Schenectady Museum, 21 left/Underwood & Underwood, p22; Getty Images/Time Life, pp left, 18/Retrofile, p16 right/Hulton Archive, p17 right/Rischgitz, p19; Library of Congress, p7; Photolibrary.com/Workbook Inc, front cover right, pp 1 right, 5 top left/Photo Researchers Inc, front cover left, pp 2 left, 4/Photonica, pp 3, 5 bottom left & right/Super Stock, pp 10, 11, 12.

ISBN 978 0 17 012566 6
ISBN 978 0 17 012561 1 (set)

Cengage Learning Australia
Level 7, 80 Dorcas Street
South Melbourne, Victoria Australia 3205
Phone: 1300 790 853

Cengage Learning New Zealand
Unit 4B Rosedale Office Park
331 Rosedale Road, Albany, North Shore NZ 0632
Phone: 0508 635 766

For learning solutions, visit cengage.com.au

Printed in Australia by Ligare Pty Ltd
10 11 12 13 14 15 16 20 19 18 17 16

THE UNIVERSITY OF MELBOURNE

Evaluated in independent research by staff from the Department of Language, Literacy and Arts Education at the University of Melbourne.

Contents

Chapter 1

A GREAT INVENTOR

Thomas Edison was a great **inventor**.
In his lifetime, he invented –
or helped to invent –
more than one thousand different things.

Many of his inventions and ideas changed the world.

If it wasn't for Thomas Edison, we might not have:

- the electric light
- sound recording
- moving pictures.

Chapter 2

EDISON AS A CHILD

Thomas Edison was born in the USA in 1847.
He was the youngest of seven children.

Edison as a child

Edison's mother, Nancy Elliot

When Edison was a child, he went to school at home. He read many books to learn about things around him.

HIS FIRST JOB

Edison started working when he was 12 years old.
His first job was selling newspapers on trains.
He did this job for two years.

When he was 14 years old,
he began his own newspaper.
He made the newspaper on one of the trains
he worked on.
No one had ever done
anything like that before!

In 1863, when Edison was 16 years old, he changed jobs.
He started working as a **telegrapher**.

men working telegraph machines

Running Words 157

a telegraph office

In 1863, there were no phones. The telegraph was the only way to send messages a long way.

Chapter 4

THE TELEGRAPH

The telegraph works by sending electrical messages down a line.

These messages are sent in **Morse code**.

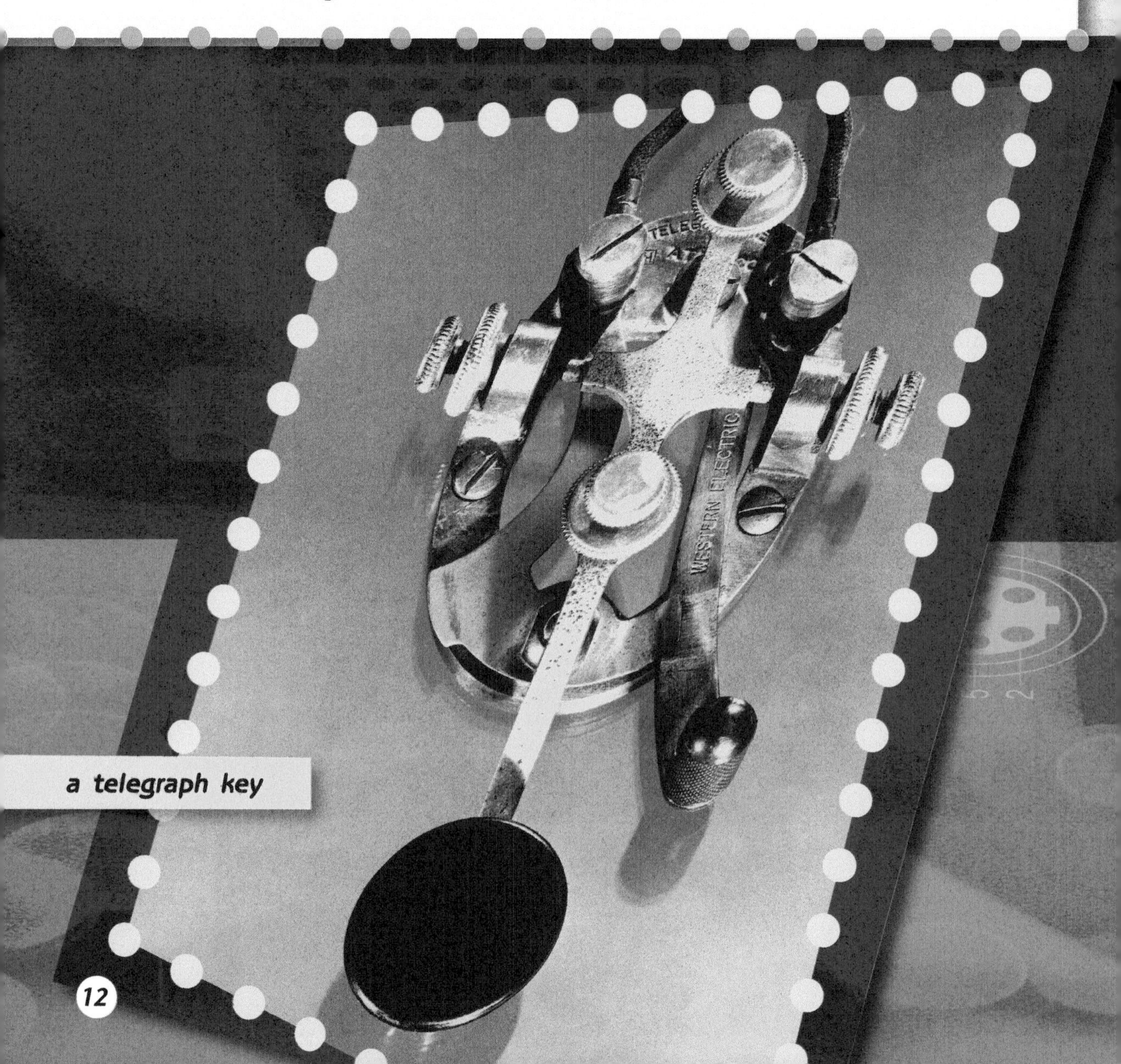

a telegraph key

Morse code uses dots and dashes
to stand for letters that make up words.

—•—— ——— ••—   —•—• •— —•

••• • —• —••   —— ——— •—• ••• •

—••• —•——   — •— •——• •——• ••

—• ——•   — •••• •   — •— —••• •—•• •

A •—
B —•••
C —•—•
D —••
E •
F ••—•
G ——•
H ••••
I ••
J •———
K —•—
L •—••
M ——
N —•
O ———
P •——•
Q ——•—
R •—•
S •••
T —
U ••—
V •••—
W •——
X —••—
Y —•——
Z ——••
full stop •—•—•—
question mark ••——••

Chapter 5

BEING DEAF

Edison became deaf when he was a child. He liked working as a telegrapher because he didn't need to hear very well to do his work.

Edison's printing telegraph

Edison's job as a telegrapher helped him to make his first big invention. He invented a telegraph machine that sent more than one telegraph at a time.

Many people say that being deaf
helped to make Edison a good inventor.
They say that he could think better
because he couldn't always hear what was going on
around him.

a phonograph with boxes of records

a phonograph

Most of Edison's inventions were to do with sound and sending messages.
These were the things he missed out on because he was deaf.

an early telephone

a kinetograph

Chapter 6

HIS LABORATORY

In 1872, Edison set up his own big **laboratory**. It was in this laboratory that he did some of his best inventing work.

Edison working in his laboratory

Edison speaking through a phonograph

He made the first sound recorder in his laboratory. He also worked on ideas that would help other people make phones, radios and moving pictures.

Chapter 7

THE ELECTRIC LIGHT

For many years, other inventors had been working on the electric light.

Edison's electric lamp

Edison's Mazda B light bulb

an early light bulb

In 1879, Edison became the first person to make the electric light work.

Edison died in 1931.
He was 84 years old.

By the time of his death, he had seen how many of his ideas and inventions had changed the world.

Glossary

inventor someone who creates or designs something

laboratory a place for scientific experiments or research

Morse code a code where letters come out as dots and dashes

telegrapher someone who works a telegraph machine

Index